First published in Great Britain in 2014 by Andersen Press Ltd.,
20 Vauxhall Bridge Road, London SW1V 2SA.
Published in Australia by Random House Australia Pty.,
Level 3, 100 Pacific Highway, North Sydney, NSW 2060.
Copyright © Tony Ross, 2014. The rights of Tony Ross to be identified as the
author and illustrator of this work have been asserted by him in accordance
with the Copyright, Designs and Patents Act, 1988.

Colour separated in Switzerland by Photolitho AG, Zürich.
Printed and bound in Italy by Grafiche AZ, Verona.

10 9 8 7 6 5 4 3 2

British Library Cataloguing in
Publication Data available.
ISBN 978 1 78344 025 2

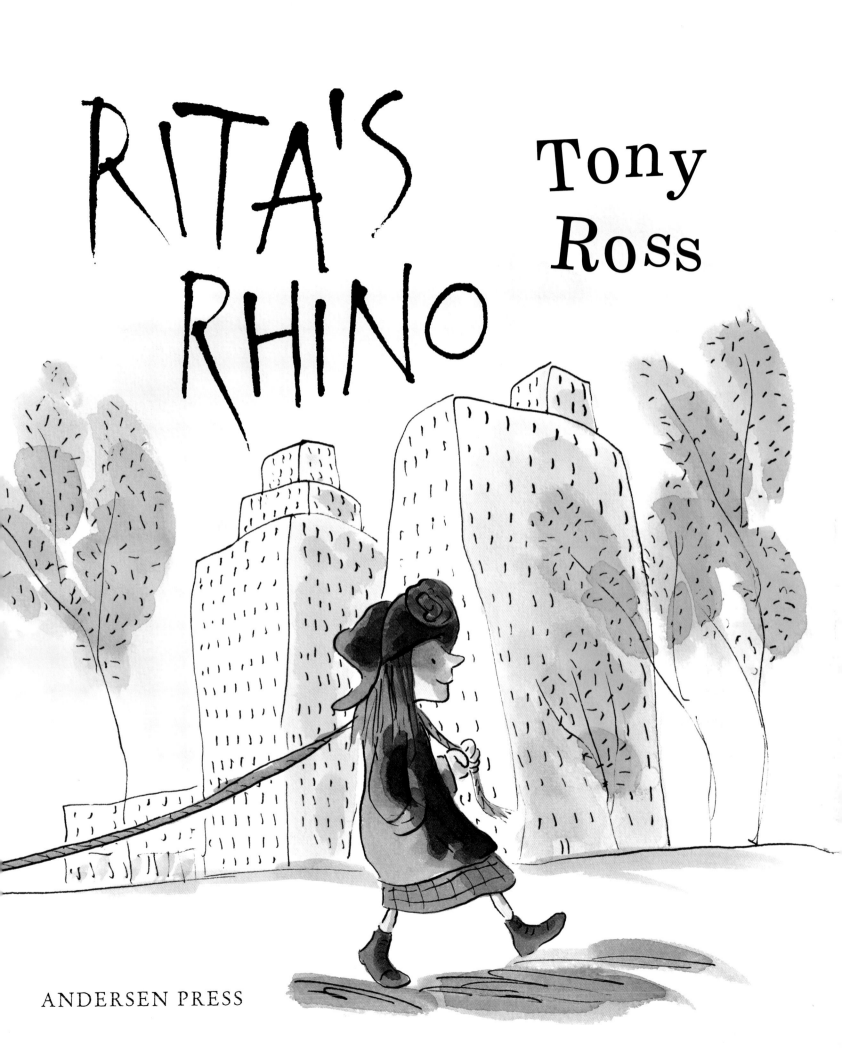

RITA'S RHINO

Tony Ross

ANDERSEN PRESS

When Rita asked for a pet, her mum said, "NOOOOOOO! Pets are stinky,
greedy things. You have to clean up after them and take them for walks."
"I'll do that," said Rita. "PLEASE!"
"All right," said Mum, "you can have a very little pet."

A few days later, Mum gave Rita a jar.
"Meet your new pet flea, Harold," she said.
"Poo, I can't even see him!" Rita snorted.

"Frogs make wonderful pets," said Uncle Eric, handing Rita a tadpole.
"Sometimes, if you kiss them, they turn into princes."
"I don't want a prince," frowned Rita. "I want a pet!"

Rita decided to find a pet for herself, so she set off to the zoo.
As she reached the rhinoceros cage, it began to rain.
"I hate the rain," groaned the rhinoceros.

"Would you like to come home with me?" asked Rita. "It's dry there."
"Yes, please," said the rhinoceros, squeezing through the bars of his cage.

Rita put her hat and coat over the rhinoceros,
so the zookeeper would not notice . . .

and the two of them walked out of the zoo.

When they reached the block where Rita lived, it was a bit
of a squeeze, getting her new pet into the lift.

It was not easy hiding a rhinoceros in a small bedroom in a small flat.
Mum brought Rita a slice of toast covered with marmalade.
As soon as she left, Rita gave it to her pet.
"I don't like toast," said the rhinoceros. "I only eat grass from Africa."
"Goodness," said Rita. "You'd better come with me."

"I only have half a bag of grass from Africa
left and it's very expensive," said the pet-shop man.
Rita frowned and emptied her purse. She looked at the rhinoceros,
"When that's gone, it'll have to be marmalade toast for you."

Sometimes, Rita began to wish she did not have a pet rhinoceros. She loved him, of course, but it would have been so much better if he were not so large. It was unpleasant hiding the piles of rhinoceros poo every day.

Sometimes, the rhinoceros missed the zoo, his comfy bed, his grass from Africa, and he always hated going up and down in the lift.

When Rita went back to school after the holidays, she took her rhinoceros with her. She left him outside with his horn stuck firmly in the ground to stop him rolling over. Rita wagged her finger at him. "Stay!" she said sternly.

"Is that a rhinoceros?" asked her teacher,
who was a bit short-sighted.
"No, Miss," said Rita. "That's my bouncy castle."

"A BOUNCY CASTLE!" whooped the
other children, rushing outside to play.

Much as he loved Rita,
the rhinoceros decided
enough was enough.

That night, he crept away, back to the zoo.

The rhinoceros was happy to be back. But as he lay on his comfy bed
and nibbled his grass from Africa, he often thought of Rita,
and when he did, he shed a little tear.

And when Rita remembered her rhinoceros, she shed a little tear too.

But every summer after that, Rita took the rhinoceros to the seaside for a few days, and they always had such a great time together that the rhinoceros was quite content to eat seaweed for a change.